D0345598

WITHDRAWN

HEARST FREE LIBRARY
ANACONDA, MONTANA

A Very Special Secret

Katharine Holabird
Based on the artwork by Helen Craig

Grosset & Dunlap

HEARST FREE LIBRARY
ANACONDA, MONTANA

To my dear friends Rollin, Courtenay, and Nick,
with tons of love—KH

GROSSET & DUNLAP
Published by the Penguin Group
Penguin Group (USA) Inc., 375 Hudson Street, New York, New York 10014, U.S.A.
Penguin Group (Canada), 90 Eglinton Avenue East, Suite 700, Toronto, Ontario, Canada M4P 2Y3
(a division of Pearson Penguin Canada Inc.)
Penguin Books Ltd, 80 Strand, London WC2R 0RL, England
Penguin Ireland, 25 St Stephen's Green, Dublin 2, Ireland
(a division of Penguin Books Ltd)
Penguin Group (Australia), 250 Camberwell Road, Camberwell, Victoria 3124, Australia
(a division of Pearson Australia Group Pty Ltd)
Penguin Books India Pvt Ltd, 11 Community Centre, Panchsheel Park, New Delhi - 110 017, India
Penguin Group (NZ), Cnr Airborne and Rosedale Roads, Albany, Auckland 1310, New Zealand
(a division of Pearson New Zealand Ltd)
Penguin Books (South Africa) (Pty) Ltd, 24 Sturdee Avenue, Rosebank, Johannesburg 2196, South Africa

Penguin Books Ltd, Registered Offices:
80 Strand, London WC2R 0RL, England

If you purchased this book without a cover, you should be aware that this book is
stolen property. It was reported as "unsold and destroyed" to the publisher, and neither
the author nor the publisher has received any payment for this "stripped book."

The scanning, uploading, and distribution of this book via the Internet or via any other
means without the permission of the publisher is illegal and punishable by law. Please purchase
only authorized electronic editions, and do not participate in or encourage electronic piracy
of copyrighted materials. Your support of the authors' rights is appreciated.

First published in Great Britain 2006 by Puffin Books.

Angelina Ballerina © 2006 Helen Craig Ltd. and Katharine Holabird. The Angelina Ballerina
name and character and the dancing Angelina logo are trademarks of HIT Entertainment Ltd.,
Katharine Holabird, and Helen Craig. Reg. U.S. Pat. & Tm. Off. Used under license by
Penguin Young Readers Group. All rights reserved. Published by Grosset & Dunlap,
a division of Penguin Young Readers Group, 345 Hudson Street, New York, New York 10014.
GROSSET & DUNLAP is a trademark of Penguin Group (USA) Inc. Printed in the U.S.A.

Library of Congress Cataloging-in-Publication Data is available.

ISBN 0-448-44332-5   10 9 8 7 6 5 4 3 2 1

Dear Diary,

Guess what? I have my very own secret clubhouse—it's the best thing since cheddar cheese!

I've named it the TREETOP CLUB and it's hidden way up in the branches of the old oak tree at the bottom of our garden, so nobody can find it. I made it all by myself (with a little help from Dad, of course).

"Your clubhouse is a bit wonky," said Dad when we finally finished hammering and banging all the boards together.

"It's still definitely the best clubhouse in all of Mouseland!" I told Dad, and I gave him a big hug.

"Well, it certainly has lots of atmosphere," Dad replied. Then he stood up and bumped his head on the ceiling. "Rats!"

After his bump Dad decided to have a nap. I ran into the house and called my very bestest friend, Alice.

"I've got something really-truly exciting to show you!" I said.

"I'll be there in a flash," said Alice. While I was waiting I did four stupendous cartwheels and two and a half almost perfect arabesques—and then Alice was banging on the door. She was that fast!

"Is the clubhouse ready?" Alice squeaked loudly.

"SHHH!" I said. "We don't want ANYONE else to know."

"Oooh, no! Specially not the snooty Pinkpaws twins!" whispered Alice, peering around.

"Too true," I agreed. "Now follow me without a squeak."

We tiptoed down to the bottom of
the garden and looked up and down to be
definitely certain that no mouselings were
following us, and then we scrambled up the
ladder. I proudly opened the door.

"Ta-da!" I said.

Alice's eyes were popping out of her head.

"It's gorgeous," she whispered.

"Definitely," I said. "Perfect for secret meetings."

"And a secret scrumptious candy box," Alice agreed.

"There's even a spyhole," I told her.

We both peeked out of the spyhole and Alice was soooo amazed. From our secret clubhouse we could see all over Chipping Cheddar—and right into grumpy old Mrs. Hodgepodge's garden next door!

"We'll be on the lookout for Mrs. Hodgepodge," I said, "so we can hide before she tells us off."

"She'll never find us here!" Alice giggled.

"Not even nosy little mouselings like my cousin Henry can find us here," I said. "It's our secret."

When we left Alice and I crossed our paws and hooted like owls: "Whooo-whoooo-whooo"—our special secret signal.

Dear Diary,

This morning I practiced all sorts of ballet positions and pliés and I twirled around and around the garden like a fairy. I have been doing absolutely tons of ballet these days because Miss Lilly's Ballet School is performing at the Chipping Cheddar Village Festival and everybody will be there—even the mayor! Miss Lilly says it will be a lovely show about gardens and flowers, and Alice and I can't wait to be gorgeous butterflies or dancing daffodil fairies!

I stopped twirling to pick some daisies, and then climbed up to the Treetop Clubhouse to make two perfect daisy crowns for me and Alice.

"Whooo-whoooo-whooo."

I peeped out of the spyhole, and there was Alice at the bottom of the ladder with a huge fat bag.

"What's that?" I asked.

"Mom had a clear out," Alice said, "and I got great stuff for our clubhouse."

Alice and I pulled the bag upstairs—and here's what we found:

3 lumpy cushions
1 wrinkly rug
2 cracked dishes

1 old fork and 2 spoons

1 dusty mirror

A flowery plastic jug with matching
glasses

"Fantastic," I said, and then we carefully
arranged our cushions on the wrinkly rug,
hung up our mirror, and put our jug and
glasses neatly in the corner. Then we plopped
down and admired our little clubhouse. It was
really-truly cozy and comfy.

"This is for you," I explained, and I
proudly gave Alice her daisy crown and put
mine on, too.

"Now we look just like real princesses!"
said Alice, smiling at herself in the mirror.

Next we opened the SECRET CANDY BOX.
I could hardly believe my eyes—inside was
a truly scrumptious cheesy nutcake, and it
was definitely the best ever because Alice

had scribbled "HOORAY FOR THE TREETOP
CLUB" in gloopy pink frosting on the top. Yum!

"It's specially for you," said Alice proudly,
and she gave me a ginormous slice. "'Cause
you're my very bestest friend and now we
have our own clubhouse."

We clinked glasses of pink lemonade
and gobbled up every bit of cake. (Cheesy
nutcake is definitely my tip-top favorite.)

Then we told our funniest jokes, and
laughed until we almost burst.

"Who is the tidiest fairy ever?" asked
Alice.

Even though I am rather clever I couldn't
think of the answer, so Alice wiggled her
nose at me. "It's the Fairy Clean—get it?"

(Tee-hee-hee-hee.)

Dear Diary,

Mom and I had a really-truly big surprise today. It all started when my little sister, Polly, was being naughty at breakfast.

"Big mouselings don't slurp their cereal," I said. Polly stuck out her tongue and spilled her Ricey Bites and milk. Soooo babyish!

"And big mouselings don't make such a horrid mess," I continued, showing her how carefully I can eat Ricey Bites. Polly let out a shriek, and Mom rushed in.

"What's all the racket about?" asked Mom, giving me a Very Stern Look (imagine!). Before I could explain, the telephone rang and Mom picked it up.

"Yes, this is Matilda Mouseling," said Mom. Then she gasped in utter amazement. "Oh, my goodness! G-g-g-ood morning, Your Majesty! Yes . . . of . . . of course. It would be a great pleasure." Mom continued speaking

ever so politely, her eyes as round as two saucers. Finally Mom said, "Good day, Your Majesty," and handed me the phone.

"Princess Sophie would like to talk to you now," Mom whispered.

I couldn't wait to chat with Princess Sophie—I hadn't seen her since I stayed at the royal palace last summer and we became tip-top friends.

"Guess what? I'm coming to Chipping Cheddar for my summer vacation—and I'll

meet all your friends!" Sophie exclaimed.

"That's the best surprise ever," I agreed.
"There's going to be a big village festival
here—so we can dance together again!"

"Stupendous," said Sophie. "I can't wait,
Angelina."

"See you soon!" I said happily. I hung up
the phone and gave Mom a hug.

"Crumbs," Mom said quietly. "We've just
invited the Princess of Mouseland to stay in
our little cottage for two whole weeks."

"Yippee!" I shouted, and I twirled round the kitchen while Polly clapped her paws. Mom washed Polly's face and wiped off the table.

"I hope the princess doesn't mind roughing it a bit," she said.

"Don't worry," I said, "Princess Sophie isn't stuck-up or fancy."

"Thank goodness," said Mom, looking at the sink full of dirty dishes.

"I'd better call Alice right away," I said, and Mom agreed.

"Secret Meeting at the TTC in five minutes!" I shouted into the phone.

"I'll get some snacks and run as fast as I can!" Alice shouted back.

"Stupendous," I said, taking the Ricey Bites as I skipped out of the door.

Dear Diary,

When Alice arrived we raced up the ladder

into the clubhouse and hung up our "Tip-Top Secret Meeting" sign on the door, just in case any nosy mouselings came round. Then we squished together on our comfy cushions and I whispered in Alice's ear. She was soooo excited to hear the news.

"Just think of it," she said, gazing out of the clubhouse window, "the Princess of Mouseland is coming here to Chipping Cheddar . . ."

"I've told her all about you," I said proudly.

"But what if she doesn't like me?" asked Alice,

munching loudly on some cheesy chips.

"Don't worry, Princess Sophie is the nicest mouseling ever," I told her.

"Won't she miss all her servants and her royal food?" asked Alice.

I shook my head.

"No way—Princess Sophie can't stand Miss Fidget, who is definitely the worst royal nanny ever," I explained, opening a packet of minty cheese balls. "And if the princess wants fancy food we can go to the Pink Peppermint Tea Parlor."

"Or buy candies at Mrs. Thimble's shop," suggested Alice.

"Perfect," I agreed. "And here's the best thing ever—Princess Sophie is going to dance in Miss Lilly's holiday show with us."

"Oooh . . . we'll all be fairies!" exclaimed Alice, spinning in front of the mirror.

"We'll be the stars," I agreed, twirling

round in front of Alice.

"We'll be the best ballerinas ever!"
Alice shouted, but then she tripped on the
wrinkly rug and crashed into me, and we
both collapsed on the cushions.

Alice picked herself up and gazed around
our cozy little clubhouse. "Where's the
princess going to sleep?" she asked, helping
herself to some minty cheese balls.

"Hmmm," I wondered. "Let's look around
the house."

We climbed down from the clubhouse
and went upstairs to my bedroom.

"Your room isn't specially princessy,"
Alice said, bouncing up and down on my bed.

"We'll get lots of flowers and buy a box
of nice chocolates," I said.

"You can't both sleep in this itsy-bitsy
bed," Alice continued stubbornly.

Just then Mom came upstairs lugging a
basket full of laundry.

"This cottage is a complete mess," she
said. "You'll have to tidy your own room to
get it ready for the princess, Angelina."

"But where am I going to sleep?" I wondered out loud.

Just then Polly crawled up the stairs, gurgling and burping.

Mom looked at Polly and then looked at me. I couldn't believe it. . . .

"Oh no!" I moaned. "Do I have to sleep with silly Polly?"

Dear Diary,

This morning Alice and I tidied my bedroom until we were completely frazzled. We picked up tons of lost pens and pencils and slippers and socks, and we taped a poster of Serena Silvertail dancing in *Mouse Lake* over the bed. Luckily we found a clever way to make everything tidy—we squished all the old tattered toys and hair ribbons and stuff right under the bed. Isn't that brilliant?

Mom came upstairs with a gorgeous new pink duvet and a fluffy new pink rug, and was she ever impressed! "Your room looks fit for a royal princess," she said with a smile.

Alice and I winked at each other, but then I felt sad. It's not fair that I have to move into Polly's messy baby room next door when my room looks so princessy. I will definitely need dear old Mousie (best cuddly toy ever) when I'm scrunched up next to my silly sister!

"Your bedroom is gorgeous now," said Alice. "We just need to add some fancy flowers."

We skipped outside to look around Mom's flower bed, but then my crabby old neighbor, Mrs. Hodgepodge, spied us and started screeching over the fence.

"Run for it, Alice!" I said (because it is definitely best to disappear whenever Mrs. Hodgepodge starts screeching!). Alice was so scared she got all tangled up in Mom's grapevine. I tried to yank Alice free, but then Mrs. Hodgepodge poked her nose through the hedge.

"I want to speak with you mouselings immediately!" Mrs. Hodgepodge said in her croaking voice. Alice's whiskers were trembling.

"We haven't done anything wrong, Mrs. Hodgepodge," I said, clutching Alice by the tail. "Honest."

"Tut-tut," croaked Mrs. Hodgepodge. "Come into my garden this minute."

I couldn't believe my furry ears. Mrs. Hodgepodge always shouts, "Stop your silly dancing!" whenever she sees me. I've never ever been allowed near her garden before, but now she was telling Alice and me to come in—imagine!

I pulled Alice out of the vine and gripped her tail tightly as Mrs. Hodgepodge opened the garden gate. We tiptoed in and looked around. Mrs. Hodgepodge has the prettiest garden I've ever seen—even though she is so old and grumpy she is definitely the best gardener in all of Chipping Cheddar.

"I want you and your little friend to take some of my prize roses for the princess," said Mrs. Hodgepodge, pointing to her flowering rose bushes.

"T-t-t-thank you," I stammered, pulling Alice along behind me.

"Of course, I can't understand why the Princess of Mouseland wants to stay in your cramped little cottage," Mrs. Hodgepodge continued, snipping prickly roses and piling them into my arms. "A royal princess should have the very best of everything."

As she talked Mrs. Hodgepodge piled more flowers on top of me—until I could hardly see where I was going.

"Be sure to give my roses lots of water and look after them properly," said Mrs. Hodgepodge when she'd finished.

"Definitely, Mrs. Hodgepodge," I replied.

"You may go now," said Mrs. Hodgepodge, opening the gate.

"Can you believe it?" I asked Alice, when we were safely back on the other side. "Mrs.

Hodgepodge didn't tell us off for once!"

"Maybe you should invite Princess Sophie to visit more often," joked Alice, rolling her eyes. Then we both started giggling and we couldn't stop.

After that Mom and I went to buy Crumbs and Cream ice cream, which is Princess Sophie's tip-top favorite. Mrs. Thimble's store was absolutely packed with customers because everybody in the village was buying pots of geraniums, tons of paint, and all the fanciest soap, polish, and wax to make their little cottages shine. On the way

home we saw the mayor, Dr. Tuttle, putting
up a huge banner in the high street:

CHIPPING CHEDDAR WELCOMES
PRINCESS SOPHIE!

The mayor and all the other grown-up mice
are making a very big fuss about Princess
Sophie, but she is actually a very shy
mouseling. She definitely hates fancy parties
and noisy crowds. In fact, Princess Sophie
is so shy she doesn't even like dancing by
herself. Luckily when we were ballet partners

at the royal palace we had the best time ever. And now Princess Sophie and I will be partners again—I can hardly wait!

Dear Diary,

It was soooo exciting when Princess Sophie arrived today. The whole village of Chipping Cheddar came out to cheer. Alice hopped up and down and squished my toes, and Henry kept squeaking, "HERE COMES THE PRINCESS!"

The Pinkpaws twins wore matching yellow outfits, and Penelope wrinkled her nose at me. "I don't know why the princess wants to stay with YOU!" she said rudely as the royal mousemobile zoomed up the hill and screeched to a stop. (Ugh. The Pinkpaws twins are definitely the most horrid mouselings in all of Mouseland.)

The driver got out and grandly opened

the door—and there was Sophie, the Princess of Mouseland, wearing a gorgeous silver cape and a golden crown. She stepped out and waved to everyone.

"Oooh!" gasped the crowd.

"Welcome, Princess Sophie," said Dr. Tuttle.

Princess Sophie thanked him, and then she turned and gave me a ginormous hug.

"Watch out," she whispered in my ear as a tall thin figure in a black cloak climbed out of the mousemobile.

"Miss Fidget!" I gasped.

"I'm the royal nanny and I always accompany the princess," Miss Fidget announced loudly to Dr. Tuttle.

Mom stepped forward, her whiskers quivering.

"I'm Angelina's mom," she said. "Very nice to meet you."

"I must inspect our rooms immediately," said Miss Fidget coldly. "Then I will unpack the princess's luggage. A royal nanny's job is never done."

"I'm afraid our cottage is quite t-t-t-tiny," stammered my mother.

"Is that so?" asked Miss Fidget, looking down her long, crooked nose.

At that moment the crowd parted and I could see Mrs. Hodgepodge waving her paws and screeching at everyone. Mrs. Hodgepodge was wearing a gruesome straw hat decorated with cabbages and gooseberries, and she scurried up next to Miss Fidget as if they were bestest friends.

"The royal nanny will stay with me," Mrs. Hodgepodge said to Mom. "My home is much more charming and comfortable than yours. And"—she looked straight at me—"I can inform Miss Fidget about the naughty little mouselings in this town."

"What a wonderful idea!" cried Dad, winking at Mom.

"Of course," said Mom politely, but I saw her give Mrs. Hodgepodge a Very Stern Look.

"CAN WE RIDE IN THE ROYAL MOUSEMOBILE NOW?" squeaked Henry.

"Shush!" whispered Mom, shaking her finger. But the princess smiled and invited us all in, so we rode back to Honeysuckle Cottage, waving at everyone just like the

royal family. It was great fun! Miss Fidget
scowled as Henry pointed and squeaked out
of the window, but Princess Sophie and I paid
no attention—we were too busy chattering to
each other in the back seat.

Dear Diary,

Honeysuckle Cottage did look a bit
squished and shabby when the gleaming royal
mousemobile zoomed up outside, but the

princess didn't seem to care. She clapped her paws and skipped around the garden while Miss Fidget peered at the cottage and marched inside.

"This hardly looks fit for a princess," she sniffed.

Mom looked on in horror as Miss Fidget poked her nose into every corner and cupboard. Polly was so scared she scampered under the kitchen table. Then Miss Fidget stomped upstairs and spent ages unpacking

the princess's silver trunk. That horrid nanny even snooped under the bed, muttering "Tsk tsk!" when she discovered my hidden, tattered toy collection. Grrrr!

Finally Miss Fidget clomped downstairs and scowled at Mom. "Your home does not meet our royal standards," Miss Fidget announced, "but it will have to do." Then she slammed the door and disappeared.

"I'm very sorry my nanny is such a terrible fusspot," said Princess Sophie quietly.

"Well, thank goodness we've finally passed the royal inspection!" said Dad. "Let's celebrate with some Crumbs and Cream ice cream."

"YES, PLEASE!" squeaked Henry as we all sat down. Just then Alice arrived, but she stood in the doorway twisting her tail.

"Anything wrong, Alice?" asked Dad.

"I've never ever actually met a real princess before . . ." said Alice nervously.

"Just call me Sophie," said the princess with a smile. "Do you like Crumbs and Cream ice cream?"

"I LOVE it!" said Alice, and she forgot about being nervous and plopped herself down next to the princess.

Dad gave Alice a huge bowl of ice cream, and I could see we'd soon have to go to Mrs. Thimble's shop for more scrumptious treats.

"I wish I could live in a palace and have servants bring me fancy royal stuff all the time," said Alice dreamily as she slurped her ice cream. "I'd wear a tiara every day and go to tons of parties."

Sophie shook her head. "Royal parties are horrid—you have to sit still for ages and eat really old smelly cheese," she said.

"Ugh," I agreed.

"But the palace is the best place ever for playing hide-and-seek," Sophie continued. "I know all the secret places in the towers and Miss Fidget can never find me."

"Oooh," gasped Alice. "Sounds stupendous."

Sophie sighed and added, "Sometimes the palace does get awfully lonely."

"It's definitely never lonely in Chipping Cheddar," I said, winking at Alice.

Alice wiggled her whiskers and asked, "What goes tock-tick, tock-tick?" And when nobody knew the answer, Alice shouted, "It's an upside-down clock, you silly-billies!"

Sophie giggled so much she got the hiccups. Henry smudged ice cream all over his nose, and Alice and I danced around the kitchen pretending to be snooty Miss Fidget. We were so funny that Mom laughed until she burst a button. Imagine!

Dear Diary,

Sharing a bed with my sister, Polly, is not exactly easy-peasy. Polly may be a tiny mouseling, but she's the worst sleeper ever. All night long she kicks me, wiggles her tail, and tickles me with her whiskers. In the morning I am completely frazzled.

"Ballerinas need lots of rest," I explained to Mom. "So I think I'd better not sleep with Polly anymore."

"Poor Angelina," said Mom. "You'll have to put up with it for a while longer." Grrrr!

Dear Diary,

Mom says Sophie is the best guest ever because she has such royal manners. (I definitely have very princessy manners, too, although Mom hasn't mentioned it just yet. . . .)

"Your cottage is really cozy and sweet," Sophie told Mom today, "and your blueberry pancakes are better than any royal breakfast."

"Goodness, how very kind!" said Mom.

"Angelina's so lucky to have such a cute little sister," Sophie continued. Polly stopped banging her spoon and gazed sweetly at Sophie.

"Sometimes she's not so cute," I explained. Then silly Polly stuck out her tongue and I made a face at her. "See what I mean?"

After breakfast Sophie and I skipped

upstairs and practiced pliés.

"Will you be my partner at our ballet
performance?" I asked.

"Absolutely," agreed Sophie, and she put
on her sparkly new pink tutu and twirled
around the room with me. But then she
plopped down on the bed.

"Miss Fidget hates ballet," said Sophie
sadly. "I'm never allowed to dance at the
palace—she ruins all my fun."

Just then we heard Mrs. Hodgepodge
croaking loudly outside. "My cabbages won

all the competitions this year," she bragged.

An icy voice answered, "You obviously have extremely green paws . . ."

We peeked out of the window, and spied Mrs. Hodgepodge in her garden with the royal nanny. Sophie whispered, "Mrs. Hodgepodge knows how to keep Miss Fidget out of mischief!" And then we both hid under the pink duvet and we didn't twitch a whisker for absolutely ages!

Dear Diary,

Today Sophie and I got all dressed up to meet Alice at the Pink Peppermint Tea Parlor, but first we had to ask Miss Fidget's permission.

Sophie looked soooo princessy in her pretty violet dress, but her tail was very droopy.

"Miss Fidget is such a pain," she whispered.

"Let's go without her," I suggested.

We tiptoed off down the lane and my pesky cousin Henry followed us.

"PLE-E-E-EASE CAN I COME, TOO?" Henry begged.

"This is a special girls' tea party," I explained.

Henry tagged along and I gave him a Very Stern Look, but then Sophie said, "Henry loves cakes more than anyone . . ."

"YIPPEE!" Henry squeaked. "I'M INVITED TO TEA WITH THE PRINCESS!"

Sophie kindly held Henry's paw as we skipped along, but then we looked back and saw Miss Fidget in her black cape charging after us down Honeysuckle Lane.

"Where are you going, you naughty mouselings?" she shrieked.

"Quick!" I shouted, and we raced off down Acorn Street, up Rat Alley, in and out of Mrs. Thimble's shop, and behind Dr. Tuttle's office. We peered all around.

"The coast is clear!" I whispered, and we dashed across the village green to the Pink Peppermint Tea Parlor.

Alice was waiting for us next to a large sign that said:

"PRIVATE ROYAL TEA PARTY"

"The royal nanny won't be coming," I explained to Mrs. Tinsel, who owns the tea parlor, while Sophie and Alice looked nervously out of the window.

"Well, then, there's even more treats for you little mouselings," said Mrs. Tinsel with a smile.

"Could we try your famous strawberry scones?" asked Sophie as we sat down. "Angelina's always talking about them."

"Anything your heart desires," said Mrs. Tinsel sweetly.

Mrs. Tinsel brought us plates stacked high with strawberry scones, cream buns, and chocolate brownies. Next came a pitcher of cream, fancy curls of butter, flowery china cups, and a steaming pot of pink peppermint tea.

"Scrumptious!" I sighed.

"Stupendous!" said Sophie.

Alice and Henry's eyes popped out of their furry heads.

"And this is my special 'Princess Sophie Cake,'" said Mrs. Tinsel proudly as she

plonked a ginormous pink cake on the crowded table.

"I'm a lucky mouseling today," said Sophie happily, choosing a single scone and a curl of butter. The princess held her china cup daintily, and drank her pink peppermint tea in tiny sips.

Alice tried to chew s-l-o-w-l-y, too, but she soon forgot her princessy manners and gobbled down three scones, two slices of princess cake, and four brownies. Alice ate so fast, she smudged chocolate frosting and strawberry jam all over her best dress.

Henry gobbled even faster than Alice, and before you could count ten whiskers, all the plates were empty!

Sophie dabbed her nose with her silk handkerchief, while Alice noisily nibbled crumbs and licked her paws. Then Henry dropped his brownie on the floor and burped.

(He is definitely too babyish for girls' fancy tea parties.)

P.S.: We were all so stuffed after our Pink Peppermint Tea Parlor party that we could hardly pirouette down Honeysuckle Lane. Luckily we didn't see Miss Fidget again!

Dear Diary,

Sophie and I had tons of blueberry pancakes for breakfast today, so we'd have lots of energy for dancing.

"I can't wait to start practicing for the show," said Sophie as we changed into our tutus.

"We'll do the best dance ever!" I agreed, thinking about our gorgeous matching costumes.

"See you later, Mom!" I called out happily.

As we skipped out of the door we

bumped smack into Miss Fidget, scowling in her black cloak. "It is my duty to protect the princess," she announced, "and I will accompany her to all ballet lessons."

"Rats!" I whispered to Sophie.

Miss Fidget stared at me coldly.

"Mouselings should not be running around the village without supervision," she snapped.

I usually leap and twirl across the village green to ballet school, but today I trudged

slowly along with Sophie and Miss Fidget, who was definitely in a gruesome mood.

"The royal nanny always knows best," she reminded us. And then she said, "No giggling or dancing in the street!" Ugh. She is soooo horrid!

I was really-truly happy when we reached Miss Lilly's Ballet School.

"What a delightful surprise to have the Princess of Mouseland join us!" Miss Lilly exclaimed. She showed Sophie around the dance studio while Miss Fidget poked her nose into everything and dusted off the piano.

All the ballerinas rushed to meet Sophie and pestered her with questions, but Miss Lilly clapped her paws and said, "My darlinks, we must begin rehearsals for our new show immediately!"

There were squeaks and squeals of joy. Sophie glanced nervously at Miss Fidget, who shook her furry paws and warned, "No silliness!"

"It must be very hard to always act royal," whispered Alice sympathetically, and Sophie nodded shyly in agreement.

"We'll begin learning 'The Dance of the Bluebell Fairies' today," Miss Lilly continued.

47

"The Princess of Mouseland will be our guest star."

All the dancers cheered, and Sophie smiled because she was soooo pleased. My ears pricked up and my whiskers trembled as I waited for Miss Lilly to announce that I would be a star, too. But what Miss Lilly said next made my heart plop down into my ballet slippers.

"Alice Nimbletoes will be Princess Sophie's partner," announced Miss Lilly. "Angelina and the Pinkpaws twins danced with the princess at the royal palace last term, so this time they will be dancing—"

I couldn't hear Miss Lilly's words because I was suddenly soooo dizzy. I wished I could tiptoe away and hide under the piano. I watched through a black cloud as Alice grabbed Sophie's paws and waltzed around and around the room with her.

Priscilla and Penelope Pinkpaws were pouting and whining.

"Why can't we be dancing bluebells, too?" they argued.

"It's Alice's turn to have the special part," Miss Lilly explained.

The twins stamped their slippers and sulked in the corner.

"Angelina, my darlink, you will be leader of the dancing ladybugs," continued Miss Lilly, busily reading down her list.

"Dancing ladybugs?" My whiskers were wobbling. "What?" I asked. Everyone else was too busy jumping around with their partners to listen, and Alice was already doing dainty bluebell-fairy steps with Sophie. Henry waved and bounced happily across the room.

"MISS LILLY SAYS I CAN DANCE WITH YOU!" Henry squeaked.

"I'm not dancing," I said.

"YES, YOU ARE!" Henry squeaked even louder.

For the first time ever, I was thinking the same things as Priscilla and Penelope Pinkpaws.

"How could Miss Lilly do this to us?" asked Priscilla.

"Who wants to be a disgusting bug with polka dots?" asked Penelope.

Henry's little paw was tugging on my tail.

"I DO!" he squeaked.

P.S.: I know my heart should be full of happiness for Alice, but instead I am really-truly miserable . . . and Princess Sophie's visit doesn't seem like much fun anymore . . .

Dear Diary,

Today I had the most gruesome headache ever and had to stay in bed. I'll probably have to go to the hospital soon. Sophie brought me breakfast, just like at the royal palace, but then she went away to ballet practice with Alice and didn't come back for absolutely ages.

Dear Diary,

I had to stay in bed again today. After ballet practice Sophie and Alice brought me a surprise from Mrs. Thimble's shop.

"I know how much you LOVE licorice whiskers," said Alice, handing me a fancy box.

"Actually, I don't feel like eating anything," I said, shoving the box under my bed. Alice looked disappointed.

"We really hope you feel better soon," said Sophie, but already my whiskers were drooping, so Alice and Sophie said good-bye and tiptoed out of the door.

P.S.: I can't believe Alice and Sophie went to Mrs. Thimble's shop without me.

Dear Diary,

Today Henry came over. He gave me a get-well card from Alice and showed off his ladybug costume.

"You look silly," I told him.

"PRINCESS SOPHIE THINKS I LOOK CUTE," squeaked Henry, jumping round the bed with Alice's card. The card had a smiley face on it, and said:

Dear Angelina,

Please get well soon—we all miss you tons!

Love from your bestest friend ever,
ALICE xxxooo

After I read the card I had a nap, and that naughty little Henry found my licorice whiskers and gobbled them up! Sophie came back from rehearsals very late and chattered on about her wonderful bluebell-fairy dance with Alice.

I felt my whiskers droop and I told Sophie that I'll probably have to stay in bed until the show is over.

Dear Diary,

This morning Mom and Dad took my temperature.

"When is Dr. Tuttle coming?" I asked.

"Your temperature is normal," said Dad. "Time to go back to ballet."

I could see Dad didn't care at all about how horribly sick I was, so I put Mom's ice bag on my head and groaned until he left for work.

In the afternoon there was a knock on the door. It was Miss Lilly!

"I'm sorry you're so upset, my darlink," she said, sitting on the bed.

"Oooh, my head aches," I moaned, squinting under the ice bag.

"You're still my special star," Miss Lilly went on, "and I need your help with the show."

"I don't know how to be a stupid ladybug," I explained.

"Nonsense," replied Miss Lilly sternly. "I expect to see you at ballet school tomorrow morning dressed in your costume and ready to dance."

Then she gave me a kiss and was gone. Imagine!

Dear Diary,

Even though my legs were wobbly and my head was buzzing, I went back to ballet class this morning. That shows I'm really-truly "professional"!

"Welcome back, Angelina," said Miss Lilly, handing me my weird ladybug outfit. I put it on and stared at myself in the mirror.

Two huge green antennae popped out of the fluffy red cap on my head, and a pair of bright red wings covered in shiny black spots flopped from my shoulders. I wanted to run back to Honeysuckle Cottage, but then I saw Flora and Felicity in their fluffy yellow hornet costumes, and William dressed up as a purple dragonfly with orange antennae, and I felt a little bit better. The Pinkpaws twins

still refused to dance, and Miss Lilly was definitely not pleased.

"Ballet dancers have to do many different parts," she explained, "and each one is very important."

Just then Alice and Sophie twirled across the studio in their sparkling bluebell-fairy tutus, and we all stared at their glittering wings and gorgeous tiaras. Alice skipped over and gave me a hug.

"I wish you could be a bluebell fairy, too, Angelina," she said.

"I was the special star last time," I said bravely. "Now it's your turn."

"It's a little bit scary being the star of the show . . ." Alice whispered, and then she flitted off to line up for our rehearsal.

"Do your best, Angelina," said Miss Lilly with a wink. I took a very deep breath, and then I flapped my puffy polka-dot wings, zoomed past the yellow hornets, and did a few fancy ladybug pirouettes round the dragonfly.

"Watch this!" I shouted as I raced past Henry and the Pinkpaws twins, twirling and leaping absolutely stupendously over all the scenery flowers. I went faster and faster until all the other bugs had to run to catch up with me. Priscilla and Penelope got tired of watching and finally decided to join in, and soon they were so busy being zooming ladybugs they forgot to complain. I showed them lots of fancy ladybug stuff, and they were so impressed they followed me everywhere.

At the end of the rehearsal, Miss Lilly said, "I'm proud of the ladybugs today."

Henry hugged me and squeaked, "YOU'RE THE BEST LEADER OF BUGS EVER, ANGELINA!"

P.S.: Miss Fidget forgot to come to three rehearsals this week. Maybe things aren't so horrible after all . . .

Dear Diary,

I was soooo wrong! Today turned out to be really-truly horrid.

Sophie and I went to Mrs. Thimble's shop—and Miss Fidget spied on us.

"A village shop is no place for a royal princess," Miss Fidget grumbled.

Mrs. Thimble was delighted to see the princess, and showed off her very best sweets. Even though Miss Fidget definitely disapproved, Sophie carefully selected some scrumptious mousiepops, minty mice, and chocolate mouse-tails.

"I need extra to share with my friends," she explained to Mrs. Thimble.

"You'll ruin your teeth!" scolded Miss Fidget.

On the way home Sophie and I chatted about ballet rehearsals while Miss Fidget marched sternly behind us.

"Miss Lilly says Alice and I dance really well together now," Sophie said proudly.

"Alice is so busy dancing I never see her," I complained, but Sophie didn't seem to notice.

"I'm very lucky to have good friends like you and Alice," she continued, offering me some minty mice. Then she stopped and whispered in my ear, "Alice says maybe I can join your Treetop Club."

I could not believe my furry ears! The Treetop Club is meant to be Alice's and my very own special secret!

"Alice told you about our clubhouse?" I asked, my whiskers twitching.

Sophie was busily searching through her bag of candy.

"I promise I won't mention it to anyone else," she said.

"Alice is a real pain!" I shouted. Then I threw my candy into the bushes and ran off as fast as I could.

"Angelina, wait!" called Sophie, but I definitely didn't want to wait—not even for the Princess of Mouseland. I raced off down Honeysuckle Lane with tears streaming down my nose and Princess Sophie running after me.

In the distance I could hear Miss Fidget screeching behind us, "Help, police! The princess has run off!"

Dear Diary,

I am definitely never speaking to Alice Nimbletoes again!

After I found out she'd told our secret to Sophie, I raced home and hid away under the pink duvet in my old room. I could hear Sophie talking to Mom in the kitchen, and then Mom came upstairs.

"Angelina, what's the matter?" she asked, but I didn't even squeak. Someone started banging on the front door, and then I could hear Officer Crumble and Miss Fidget in the hallway.

"It has come to my attention that the

Princess of Mouseland has mysteriously disappeared," Officer Crumble said.

"And it's all your daughter's fault," Miss Fidget told Dad.

"Won't you please step into the kitchen?" asked Dad politely.

The police officer marched importantly into the kitchen, huffing and puffing—and there was Sophie, sipping hot chocolate with Polly.

Miss Fidget was not a bit happy about it.

"There's no respect for the royal nanny these days!" she shouted as she stomped off.

Officer Crumble tipped his helmet and apologized to Mom and Dad before he left. Then Sophie tiptoed upstairs to see me. "It was all a stupid mistake," she said tearfully. "Please don't blame Alice."

"I don't want to talk about it!" I shouted from under the duvet.

There was nothing to say. I understood everything:

1. Alice doesn't care about our secret anymore.
2. Alice doesn't need me to be her partner or friend anymore.
3. Alice is the star of the village show with Princess Sophie—and Miss Lilly thinks they dance stupendously together.
4. Alice has a new secret—she likes Sophie better than me.

Dear Diary,

I am trying to be a good leader of the
ladybugs at ballet school, but whenever
Alice and Sophie leap onstage as the sparkly
bluebell fairies, I don't feel like flying around
on my polka-dot wings anymore.

Sophie twirls and giggles with all the
other dancers now because Miss Fidget
has stopped coming to the rehearsals. Miss
Fidget is so busy visiting garden centers and
discussing rose-rot (whatever that is!) with
Mrs. Hodgepodge that she doesn't have much
time for spying anymore. But she still peers
into Honeysuckle Cottage on her way home
sometimes and gives Polly a terrible fright.

Before Princess Sophie came to Chipping
Cheddar I really-truly thought she was my
special friend, but now Sophie always dances
with Alice while I have to buzz around with
the other ladybugs. When Alice comes to

play at Honeysuckle Cottage I go upstairs to read Mouseland Mysteries while Alice tells jokes to Sophie in the kitchen. Mom says it's hard to share your friends, but Mom doesn't realize that Alice likes Sophie better than me—and that Sophie likes Alice best, too. There isn't any room left for me . . . or for sharing.

Dear Diary,

Tomorrow is the village festival. I wish I was excited about it like everyone else. Mom says that bluebells and ladybugs are all the same and she's coming to cheer and enjoy the show. Miss Lilly says it's the best dance ever and we should all be very proud of ourselves. Alice and Sophie are definitely thrilled, and even Henry is a happy mouseling—he thinks being a ladybug is just like being Batmouse with polka dots! I'm the only one who doesn't seem to be having much fun. . . .

Dear Diary,

Alice came over this morning to get ready for the performance.

While I struggled into my antennae and floppy wings I could hear her whispering with Sophie. My whiskers started trembling, and I tiptoed out of the cottage and climbed into the Treetop Clubhouse. Alice and Sophie called my name, but I didn't care. The show would be better without me, I decided.

Just then Dad stuck his head through the crooked clubhouse door and banged his nose. "Rats!" Dad shouted. He slowly climbed inside and squished down next to me.

"How about a hug?" Dad asked.

"Definitely not," I said, scowling like Miss Fidget. But then I burst into tears.

"I don't feel like dancing," I said, sniffling on Dad's shoulder.

"Oh dear," said Dad, "you must be very upset."

I nodded and wiped my nose.

"Still, you don't want to let Miss Lilly down," Dad reminded me. "Or the other ladybugs . . ."

"They would be in a real mess," I admitted.

"The show must go on," said Dad, and I knew he was right.

"I guess I'd better run," I said. Then I gave Dad a hug, and dashed off with my antennae flapping.

"Thank goodness you're here," said Miss
Lilly as I joined everyone backstage.

Just then the band began to play and the
curtains opened. I smiled bravely at Miss
Lilly, and then I zoomed on to the stage and
did a few extra twirls and super-high leaps
over the scenery flower beds. After that,
Alice and Sophie did their special dance. I
could see that the noise and bright lights
made Sophie nervous, and she stumbled and

forgot a few bluebell-fairy steps, which was not very professional. Then the hornets and the dragonfly did a funny waltz and the ladybugs zoomed onstage and leaped over the flowers again. Penelope lost her temper and flew off by herself (I bet Miss Lilly will have a Serious Talk with her later . . .) and poor Henry dropped one of his antennae, but he kept dancing and I was very proud of him.

At the end of the performance the

ladybugs and other insects lined up behind the bluebell fairies, and we all bowed together. Then Miss Lilly stepped on to the stage with a big smile. "Will the leader of the ladybugs please come forward?" she asked.

Gasp! That was me. I was so surprised I almost tripped over Henry's tail.

"During the holidays, Angelina's friends have been keeping a very special secret," Miss Lilly announced to the audience. My antennae started shaking as Alice and Sophie also stepped to the front of the stage and stood beside me.

"Today we are celebrating the Village Friendship Award," said Alice proudly, "and my friend Angelina is the winner because she is definitely the bestest, kindest, most understanding mouseling in all of Mouseland."

I almost fell off the stage in my floppy ladybug costume.

"I'm soooo lucky that Angelina is my very good friend, too," Princess Sophie continued, "because Angelina always helps other dancers. Angelina showed me how to do ballet and invited me to visit Chipping Cheddar—she even let me stay in her new pink bedroom!"

The audience stood up and clapped while Sophie and Alice (who are now both my best friends ever) put a shiny gold medal round my neck and gave me a ginormous hug. Imagine!

Dear Diary,

Today was Princess Sophie's last day here. We had tons of blueberry pancakes for breakfast, and then Alice came over to say good-bye.

"Let's go outside," I said to Sophie. "Alice and I have a surprise for you."

We all skipped down to the oak tree at the bottom of the garden, and Alice placed a daisy crown on Sophie's head and we hooted together.

"Whooo-whoooo-whooo!"

"Princess Sophie, you are now a member of the Treetop Club," I announced.

Then we all scrambled up the ladder and I opened the door. The clubhouse was full of streamers and balloons.

"It's my dream come true," said Sophie, stepping inside.

Alice opened up the Secret Candy Box

and handed out treats, and we all sipped
pink lemonade and told silly jokes. Then we
showed Sophie our spyhole, and she gasped

when she peeped into Mrs. Hodgepodge's garden.

"Miss Fidget is back and she's looking for me!" Sophie whispered.

We all crept up to the spyhole and pressed our ears next to it, and we could hear Miss Fidget and Mrs. Hodgepodge in the garden below.

"No more nannying!" Miss Fidget was saying. "From now on the princess will have to manage without me."

Sophie's whiskers were wobbling and we stared at each other in amazement.

"Quite right," croaked Mrs. Hodgepodge. "I don't know how you put up with those naughty little mouselings for so long!"

"Next week 'Fidget's Fantastic Flower Shop' will open in Chipping Cheddar," continued Miss Fidget, "then everyone will know my secret."

Sophie and Alice and I could not believe
our furry ears.

"Imagine!" whispered Princess Sophie,
and we all had a terrible fit of the giggles.
We giggled so much we got the hiccups and
had to stand on our heads. Then we did a
ladybug waltz around the clubhouse—and we
all decided that it was definitely the best
Treetop Club party ever.